THE GREEN
TOENAILS GANG

By Marjorie and Mitchell Sharmat:

Olivia Sharp, Agent for Secrets
THE PIZZA MONSTER
THE PRINCESS OF THE FILLMORE STREET SCHOOL
THE SLY SPY

By Marjorie Weinman Sharmat:

Nate the Great
NATE THE GREAT
NATE THE GREAT AND THE BORING BEACH BAG
NATE THE GREAT AND THE LOST LIST
NATE THE GREAT AND THE MISSING KEY
NATE THE GREAT AND THE PHONY CLUE
NATE THE GREAT AND THE SNOWY TRAIL
NATE THE GREAT STALKS STUPIDWEED
NATE THE GREAT AND THE STICKY CASE
NATE THE GREAT GOES UNDERCOVER
NATE THE GREAT AND THE FISHY PRIZE

THE SON OF THE SLIME WHO ATE CLEVELAND

By Mitchell Sharmat:

COME HOME, WILMA
GREGORY, THE TERRIBLE EATER
A GIRL OF MANY PARTS
REDDY RATTLER AND EASY EAGLE
SHERMAN IS A SLOWPOKE
THE SEVEN SLOPPY DAYS OF PHINEAS PIG

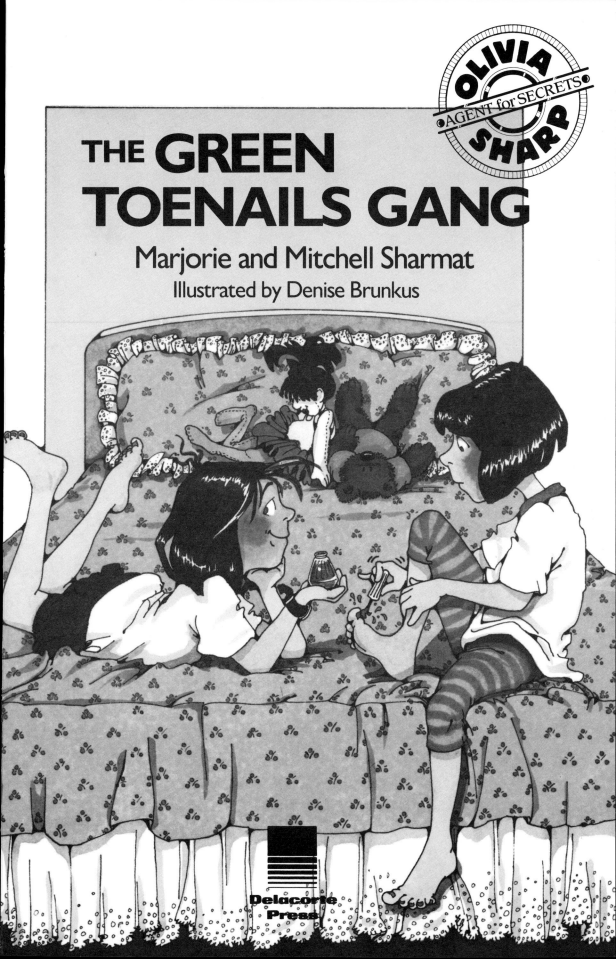

OLIVIA SHARP
AGENT for SECRETS

THE GREEN TOENAILS GANG

Marjorie and Mitchell Sharmat
Illustrated by Denise Brunkus

Delacorte Press

For Lisa Wiczer Sharmat
WELCOME
to the family
—M.S. and M.S.

For my boyfriend
Wayne
—D.B.

Published by
Delacorte Press
Bantam Doubleday Dell Publishing Group, Inc.
666 Fifth Avenue
New York, New York 10103

Library of Congress Cataloging in Publication Data

Sharmat, Marjorie Weinman.
The Green Toenails Gang / by Marjorie and
Mitchell Sharmat ; illustrated by Denise Brunkus.
p.   cm. — (Olivia Sharp, agent for secrets)
Summary: Wealthy Olivia Sharp, agent for secrets,
uncovers several secrets on a trip to Carmel,
California, to help a friend become a member of an exclusive club.
ISBN 0-385-30248-7
[1. Secrets—Fiction.   2. Clubs—Fiction.
3. Friendship—Fiction.]   I. Sharmat, Mitchell.
II. Brunkus, Denise, ill.   III. Title.   IV. Series:
Sharmat, Marjorie Weinman.   Olivia Sharp, agent for secrets.
PZ7.S5299Gq   1991
[E]—dc20   90-3645
                                              CIP
                                               AC
Manufactured in the United States of America

July 1991

10 9 8 7 6 5 4 3 2 1

LBM

My name is Olivia Sharp. I'm an agent for secrets. I'm getting kind of famous in my neighborhood. I work out of an office in my penthouse on top of Pacific Heights in San Francisco.

My best friend is Taffy Plimpton. She used to live in my building on the fourth floor. Not anymore. She moved to Carmel, California. I miss her a lot.

Right after Taffy left I did two things. First I got an owl I named Hoot. Hoot keeps me company, but she's no Taffy Plimpton.

Then I went into the agent-for-secrets business.

One day I was sitting in my favorite white fluffy chair looking out across San Francisco Bay and smoothing Hoot's feathers. My chauffeur, Willie, came into the room. "A letter for you, Boss," he said.

The envelope was postmarked Carmel, California. I knew the letter was from Taffy. I tore open the envelope and read:

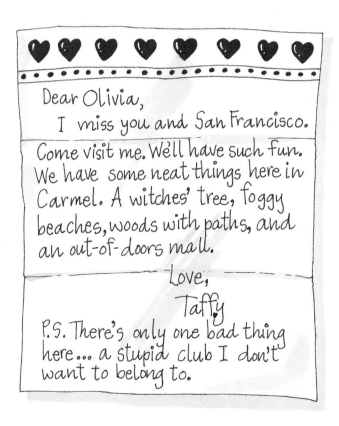

Dear Olivia,
    I miss you and San Francisco. Come visit me. We'll have such fun. We have some neat things here in Carmel. A witches' tree, foggy beaches, woods with paths, and an out-of-doors mall.
                    Love,
                        Taffy
P.S. There's only one bad thing here... a stupid club I don't want to belong to.

I read Taffy's letter again. Agents for secrets have to know how to read between the lines. That's how they learn what's really important. I knew that Taffy's P.S. was more important than the rest of her letter. It told me that Taffy, secretly, wanted help.

Taffy was in luck. Her best friend is an agent for secrets. I decided to take her case.

I got up from my chair and went into the kitchen. My housekeeper, Mrs. Fridgeflake, was busy making radishes look like rosebuds.

"I'm going to pop down to Carmel and visit Taffy Plimpton for the weekend," I said.

"Did she invite you?"

"Yes." I showed her Taffy's letter.

"I see she didn't invite Hoot," said Mrs. Fridgeflake. "That's good. Hoot wouldn't want to miss the Saturday cartoons. They're going to show her favorite tomorrow. *The Owl and the Pussycat.*"

Hoot hooted. It was settled.

I went into my office and grabbed my red telephone. It's the one I use for business.

I called Taffy. She answered.

I said, "This is Olivia. I got your letter and I'm taking your case. I'm on my way."

I hung up. I never give a client a chance to protest.

Taffy was my first out-of-town client.

I started a file on her:

TAFFY PLIMPTON
OF
CARMEL, CALIFORNIA,
NEEDS ME

I rang for Willie. "We're going to Carmel for the weekend," I said. "Pack fast and bring the limo around."

I stuffed Taffy's file and some clothes into an overnight bag and dropped a bunch of my business cards into my pocketbook.

Then I flung my boa over my shoulders, said good-bye to Hoot and Mrs. Fridgeflake, and dashed out the door. I took the elevator to the ground floor.

E.J. was standing in front of the
building. He's the boy who moved into
Taffy's old apartment.

"Going somewhere, Liver?" he asked.

I do *not* like that nickname!

"The name is Olivia," I said as I
stepped into the limo and slammed the
door.

"You said Carmel, Boss?" Willie asked as we rolled out of the courtyard through the iron gates and onto Steiner Street.

"Yes. We're going to Taffy Plimpton's house," I said. "She needs help."

"Life has gotten more interesting since you went into business, Boss," Willie said as he pulled on the visor of his cap.

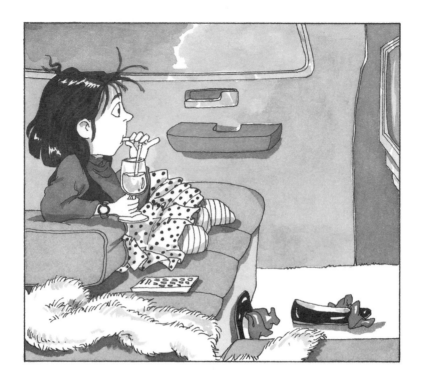

It takes only a couple of hours to drive from San Francisco to Carmel. It's a boring ride with lots of traffic.

I passed the time watching TV and sipping orange juice in the back of the limo.

Willie found Taffy's house even though it was pretty dark when we got there.

He parked the limo in the circular driveway while I ran up the front steps.

I pressed the bell. Chimes rang out.

Taffy flung open the door. She looked just the same. Big eyes. Big freckles. Big smile. And red hair as soft and fluffy as my boa right after it comes from the cleaner's.

"Your phone call . . ." she began.

I said, "You have a problem that you're trying to keep secret. I'm now an agent for secrets. Here's my card. I'm also here as your best friend. I don't have a card for that."

"It's great that you came," Taffy said. "But I don't have a secret problem."

I know a problem when I read one. But I decided it could wait.

I motioned toward the limo. "Willie helps me with my cases. And my owl, Hoot, gives me advice. She couldn't make it this weekend. She had other plans."

Taffy gave me a funny look, then waved to Willie. "Willie can stay in the guesthouse and you can stay here with us."

Taffy's mother and father asked a lot of questions.

I told them my parents were in Tibet but they were coming home next week and I could hardly wait.

I told them that a boy named E.J. had moved into their old apartment. I didn't tell them that he calls me "Liver."

After supper Taffy and I took a walk along the beach. Her house overlooks the water. The tide was out. The fog was coming in.

I got down to business.

"I know you want to belong to a club that won't let you in," I said.

Taffy picked up a seashell. "It's a stupid club, just like I wrote you."

"Taffy darling, lots of clubs are stupid. Like, if three people have green toenails they form a green toenails club and leave everybody else out."

"Hey, that's a great idea!" Taffy said. "Let's you and I form a green toenails club and we'll leave everybody else out. We'll be the Green Toenails Gang!"

"Taffy," I said, "how can we be a gang if there are only two of us?"

"Oh."

"I suppose we could ask Willie."

Taffy hugged me. "Terrific. We've got a club. All we need is the green polish."

I knew that this club wouldn't solve Taffy's problem. "When Willie and I go home," I said, "you'll be the only one in town with green toenails and you still won't be a member of the other club."

"Oh."

"Tell me, does this other club have a name?"

"Its name and everything else about it are a secret," Taffy said. "All I know is that each member wears a T-shirt with her first initial on it, printed big."

"Who belongs? What are they like?" I asked.

"There are five members and they all live here in my neighborhood. Millicent, Jasmine, Nettie, Leah, and Katrina. They say they're my friends, but they didn't ask me to join their club." Taffy looked hurt.

That night, before I went to bed, I made a note in my file.

PROBLEM:
THE SECRET FIVE

AIM:
THE SECRET SIX

The next morning I had Willie bring the limo around.

"Show me where Millicent, Jasmine, Nettie, Leah, and Katrina live," I said to Taffy.

Taffy gave Willie directions. We started cruising the neighborhood.

Suddenly Taffy cried, "Stop! There they are!"

I saw five girls ahead, riding bicycles. Each girl was wearing a T-shirt with an initial on it. I immediately knew who each girl was. *M* was for Millicent, *N* was for Nettie, *K* was for Katrina, *L* was for Leah, and *J* was for Jasmine.

"Don't stop," I said to Willie. "Follow those bicycles! Follow those T-shirts!"

"Why?" Taffy asked.

"Isn't it obvious?" I said. "They're a *bicycle* club! Let's see where they're going."

Willie cruised behind the girls. Suddenly he stopped. "Can't go any farther, Boss," he said. "They're going into the woods on a narrow path."

"Wait here," I said.

Taffy and I jumped out of the limo and ran after the bicycle riders. But they were too fast for us.

As we walked back to the limo, I was thinking. *Those girls are too fast for my feet, but they aren't too fast for my head.* I had a plan.

Back in the limo I announced, "We're going to the mall."

At the mall I bought a pretty neck-
lace of seashells for Mrs. Fridgeflake. I
bought picture postcards for my friends
Duncan, Desiree, Sheena, and Mortimer,
and an ankle bracelet for Hoot. But I
didn't find what I really wanted.

"Is there a bicycle shop around here?"
I asked Taffy.

"Down the hill and one street over,"
Taffy said.

At the bicycle store I took out five
hundred dollars and said, "I'll take two
of whatever this buys."

Sometimes it's nice to be rich.

Sometimes it isn't.

This time it was.

We left the shop with the two bikes.

I said, "Here's *your* present, Taffy. Have a bicycle. Either one."

"But I don't know how to ride," Taffy said.

"I know that. I'll teach you. I learned from a pro last summer on Nantucket Island."

Taffy and I walked the bikes down the hill to the bicycle path along Monterey Bay.

Then, with Willie on one side of her and me on the other, Taffy started her lesson.

W obble, tilt, twist, wobble, tilt, twist, wobble.

"You can do it," I said.

If you tell someone they can do something, they think you think they can do it, and they never find out that you were just guessing.

It worked.

"Whee! This is fun," Taffy said as Willie and I finally let go.

If I ever have to give up the agent-for-secrets business, maybe I'll become a bike instructor.

Taffy and I headed north on the bicycle path toward Taffy's house. Willie followed with the limo on the road that ran alongside the path.

After we ate lunch, I said, "Now you're ready."

"You know me. I'm always ready," Taffy said. "What am I ready to do this time?"

"To ride your bike in front of the girls. The reason you weren't invited into their club is that you couldn't ride a bicycle."

The first house we rode to was Jasmine's. We didn't see anybody, and no one noticed us.

Next stop was at Millicent's.

We were in luck! Millicent was in front of her house with the other four girls. A full audience.

Taffy pedaled ahead toward the girls, shouting, "Look at me!" She screeched to a stop in front of them.

The girls stared at her bike and ran their fingers over it.

Good sign. Taffy was practically a member of the club. This case was practically over.

Taffy beckoned to me.

I pedaled over.

"Olivia," Taffy said, "I want you to meet Jasmine, Nettie, Millicent, Leah, and Katrina."

"Hi," I said.

"Your name is Olivia?" Nettie asked.

"Yes."

Nettie looked at Jasmine, who looked at Millicent, who looked at Katrina, who looked at Leah, who looked at me.

Was there something wrong with my name?

"Where do you live, Olivia?" Katrina asked.

I pointed in the direction of San Francisco. "North of town," I said, and I rode away.

I wanted to leave Taffy alone with the girls. I went back to her house and waited on her front steps.

At last I saw her, bicycling toward me and smiling.

"Quick, tell me," I said. "They asked you to join their club, didn't they?"

"Not yet," Taffy said. "But they invited me to go bike riding with them Monday after school."

"You see?" I said. "That's when they'll invite you to become a member. Remember to act surprised when they tell you that their secret club is a bicycle club."

I made a note:

CASE WILL
CLOSE MONDAY.

We went inside and drank lemonade.

The phone rang.

"Maybe it's them and they're asking me right now," Taffy said.

Taffy grabbed the phone and said hello. She listened. She looked puzzled.

Then she handed the receiver to me. "It's for you," she said.

Now *I* was puzzled.

"Hello?"

"Hello, Olivia? This is Nettie. You just met me and my friends, remember?"

"I remember."

"Well, my friends and I have a secret club. Only our members know what the secret is."

That's what she thinks!

Nettie went on. "Olivia, we knew the moment Taffy introduced you to us that we wanted *you* in our club."

"Me?"

"You."

"Why?"

"That's a secret, and I can't tell you our club secret until you join."

"Look," I said, "I already know your secret. You're a bicycle club. It isn't the most original secret, I might add—"

Nettie interrupted. "We're *not* a bicycle club."

I hadn't counted on this.

Nettie pressed on. "If you join, then Taffy will be one step nearer to being asked in. We like her, but we're not ready for her."

"What do you mean?"

"Can't tell you unless you join. Well . . . ?"

"I'm thinking, I'm thinking."

I hung up.

"Small problem," I said to Taffy. "They want *me* to join their club."

"They want *you*?" Taffy looked grim. "They don't even know you, and they like you better."

"They don't like me better. Count on it."

I thought about what Nettie had told me. *The moment Taffy introduced you to us, we knew we wanted you in our club.*

Why so fast?

What did they know about me? Taffy told them my name, that's all.

Olivia.

Was there something about *Olivia* that fitted in with their secret?

I wrote down my name in my note-
book. Then I wrote down the girls'
names.

Did all the names have something in
common?

Nothing I could see.

What else did Nettie say?

She said if I joined, then Taffy would
be *one step nearer to being asked in.*

What did that mean?

I rewrote the names in a different or-
der.

Nothing clicked.
Something clicked!

I rushed to the door. "I'll be back."

I found Willie in the driveway washing the limo.

"To Jasmine's house," I said.

On the way over I kept thinking, *Now I can help my best friend.*

I rang Jasmine's doorbell. She had chimes too.

When she answered, I stepped inside and made myself comfortable on her couch.

"I know your secret," I said. "*You* probably started this club. Then you invited Katrina to join. Then Leah. Then Millicent. Then Nettie. And now me. You each wear a T-shirt with your first initial on it. *J. K. L. M. N.* And if I join you'll have an *O.* But Taffy's a *T* and she can't get in until you have a *P, Q, R,* and *S.*"

I started to fluff my boa, but then remembered I wasn't wearing it.

"You're an *Alphabet Club*!" I said.

Jasmine gasped.

I said, "I know your secret but you didn't tell me. Therefore I don't have to keep it."

"Does this mean you're not joining the club?"

"I don't live in Carmel," I said. "I live in San Francisco."

"That's okay. We need an *O* badly."

I *hate* clubs! All those secret handshakes and pins and meetings and all that rot. And now every time I came down to Carmel I'd be stuck with all that stuff. But I had to join. I had to give them an *O*.

"I'll join," I said, "if you invite Taffy in. What good is a club that makes somebody feel left out and unhappy?"

"Taffy will get in," Jasmine said. "But it'll take time."

I stood up. I put my hands on my hips. *"Rush it!"* I said.

Jasmine looked blank.

I, an agent for secrets, knew how to rush it.

I opened my pocketbook, fished out one of my cards, and scribbled something on it. I underlined five letters and gave the card to Jasmine. "Read this carefully," I said, "and get back to us. I'll keep your secret for twenty-four hours."

Jasmine looked at my card. "I'll see what I can do," she said.

Willie drove me back to Taffy's.

She was waiting for me. "What's up?" she asked.

"Wait and see," I said. "Trust me."

The next day Taffy and I went to the Witches' Tree and had a picnic lunch under it.

We went for a walk in the woods.

We watched the fog gather over the Pacific Ocean.

Then I packed to go home.

I looked at my watch. The twenty-four hours were almost up.

The telephone rang.
"It's for you this time," I said.
Taffy picked up the receiver.
She said the following:
"Hello." (Pause)
"Really?" (Pause)
"Yes!" (Pause)
"What?" (Pause)
"Well, I'll get used to it." (Pause)
"Bye."
She hung up. She shouted, "It was Jasmine. She asked me into the club and I said yes!"
Success!

"They're going to tell me their secret at the next meeting."

I hugged Taffy. "Aren't you glad we didn't start the Green Toenails Gang?"

"You bet," Taffy said.

I picked up my overnight bag.

"Just one thing," Taffy said. "Jasmine called me 'Plimp.' Isn't that a silly nickname?"

"No, I rather like it," I said.

My visit was over, my client was happy. Now all I had to do was go home and face E.J. and my own nickname.

Willie brought the limo around.

"So long, best friend," Taffy said.

"So long, Plimp," I said.

Willie started the limo and we rolled out of the circular driveway.

I pulled my file on the case.
I wrote:

> THE SECRET FIVE GOT
> MY MESSAGE:
>
> TAFFY "PLIMP" PLIMPTON.
>
> WHY DIDN'T THEY THINK OF
> THAT THEMSELVES?
>
> I GUESS IT TAKES AN AGENT
> FOR SECRETS TO FIGURE OUT
> THESE THINGS.
>
> CASE CLOSED.

Willie turned north, and we drove toward San Francisco.

I was glad I would never have to ask him to paint his toenails green.

About the Authors

MITCHELL SHARMAT and MARJORIE WEINMAN SHARMAT have written several children's books together and numerous books individually. The award-winning authors have now teamed up to create an original and amazing new series about Olivia Sharp, a helpful, problem-solving grade-school heroine who is in business for herself as an agent for secrets.

Marjorie Sharmat was born and grew up in Portland, Maine. She has been writing since age eight and is the author of nearly a hundred books. She is probably best known as the creator of the world-famous sleuth Nate the Great. Mitchell Sharmat, a native of Brookline, Massachusetts, and a graduate of Harvard, is active in real estate and stock market investments when he's not writing books. His wildly popular *Gregory, the Terrible Eater,* a Reading Rainbow featured selection, has become a children's classic.

The Sharmats live in Tucson, Arizona. They have two grown sons, Craig and Andrew.

About the Illustrator

DENISE BRUNKUS has illustrated several books for young children. She lives in Hunterdon County, New Jersey, with her husband, young daughter, and otter hound.